Mabel Beecher

Future Teacher

Cari Best

illlustratated by
Lisa Hunt

Sky Pony Press
New York

For Mrs. Pellman:
best teacher and friend ever, who showed me the way.
— C.B.

For Mum and Dad:
thank you for teaching me to follow my dreams,
and to Ant for helping me follow them.
— L.H.

Text copyright © 2018 by Cari Best
Illustrations copyright © 2018 by Lisa Hunt

Sky Pony Press books may be purchased at special discounts for sales promotion, corporate gifts, fund-raising, or educational purposes. Special editions can also be created to specifications. For details, contact the Special Sales Department, Sky Pony Press, 307 West 36th Street, 11th Floor, New York, NY 10018 or info@skyhorsepublishing.com.

Sky Pony® is a registered trademark of Skyhorse Publishing, Inc.®, a Delaware corporation.

Visit our website at www.skyponypress.com.

10 9 8 7 6 5 4 3 2 1

Manufactured in China, March 2018. This product conforms to CPSIA 2008

Library of Congress Cataloging-in-Publication Data

Names: Best, Cari, author. | Hunt, Lisa (Lisa Jane), 1973- illustrator.
Title: Mabel Beecher : future teacher / Cari Best ; illustrated by Lisa Hunt.
Description: New York : Sky Pony Press, [2018] | Summary: "When Mrs. Ampersand announces that she'll be leaving for the rest of the year, and the substitute is just not as good, Mabel decides to take matters into her own hands"-- Provided by publisher. |
Identifiers: LCCN 2017054925 (print) | LCCN 2018001526 (ebook) | ISBN 9781510720725 (eb) | ISBN 9781510720718 (print : alk. paper) | ISBN 9781510720725 (ebook)
Subjects: | CYAC: Teachers--Fiction. | Kindergarten--Fiction. | Schools--Fiction.
Classification: LCC PZ7.B46579 (ebook) | LCC PZ7.B46579 Mab 2018 (print) | DDC [E]--dc23
LC record available at https://lccn.loc.gov/2017054925

Print ISBN: 978-1-5107-2071-8
EBook ISBN: 978-1-5107-2072-5

Cover illustration by Lisa Hunt
Cover design by Kate Gartner

You won't believe what happened!
The best teacher EVER, Mrs. Ampersand,
had to leave school before kindergarten was over.
She was supposed to stay forever.

"A baby is born every eleven seconds in the United States,"
she announced, "and mine is coming . . .
UNEXPECTEDLY SOON!"

This is Mrs. Ampersand on the day she left school with Mr. Ampersand.

"I am as big as a blue whale!" She laughed. "That's the biggest mammal on earth."

She gave each of us a lightning fast hug,
including one for me, Mabel Beecher.

Mrs. Ampersand was funny and smart and the best reader when we had story time. She made hard words like this: AM-PER-SAND seem easy. "Just sound them out," she'd say.

And she gave us Popsicles every Friday if we tried hard all week.

AM-PER-SAND

She made us feel brave when the lights went out during a storm.

"Did you know that Thomas Edison was afraid of the dark before he invented the light bulb?" she told us last week.

At our last assembly, our principal, Mr. Fairchild, said, "Mrs. Ampersand is a teacher and a half. We'll miss her and her teachable moments every day for the rest of the school year."

Some of my friends cried. . . .
That reminded me of one of Mrs. Ampersand's teachable moments.
"Just think, people," I told everyone. "If we were traveling in outer space,
tears wouldn't roll down our cheeks because there is no gravity up there."

That night, I told my mom and dad, "I am more than slightly worried about how our class will survive kindergarten without Mrs. Ampersand."

"You'll be fine, Mabel," they said. "Just use your noodle."

I didn't tell them that I was more than slightly jealous that Mrs. Ampersand's new baby would be seeing her every day— while I would be seeing a substitute.

Who, by the way, is here today. Her name is Mrs. Windbag. Albert Blunt immediately started making mouth noises and fake sneezing.

PPPUURRRPP!

Mrs. Ampersand told us to be kind to every living thing. Mrs. Windbag is a living thing. So I said, 'Albert, you are disappointing Mrs. Ampersand by being rude.'

Just like that, Albert stopped. No one wanted to disappoint Mrs. Ampersand.
Not even Albert Blunt.

Mrs. Windbag started telling us all about natural gas. She didn't even ask what we'd been learning the day Mrs. Ampersand left. Mammals!

"Millions of years ago, animals and plants were buried deep under the earth and got so hot, they gave off fumes," said Mrs. Windbag for the forty-seventh time.

I felt like making mouth noises. Or flying away like a bat.
But I didn't. I was kind to Mrs. Windbag for over an hour.

Then I thought of something else Mrs. Ampersand told us:

"No question is ever not important enough to ask."

So I raised my hand.

"Can we please talk about something else now?" I asked.

Guess what Mrs. Windbag said?

"Be my guest, Mabel."

So I stood up and told the class everything un-boring I knew about bats.

"There are over one thousand kinds of bats," I said. "The biggest is the size of a pigeon. The smallest is the size of a bee."

At recess, I showed everyone how to hang like a bat.
Even Mrs. Windbag tried it.

We got back to our classroom just in time, because a storm was brewing. The lights went out again. Only, Mrs. Windbag didn't make us feel brave like Mrs. Ampersand had.

"Darkness is the absence of light," said Mrs. Windbag with authority.

That didn't help Marian Saltpeter who was shaking like a leaf. And big Oliver Crumb who started counting backward from five hundred to keep himself from biting his nails.

So I used my noodle and told the class a poem that my grandma once taught me:

"The baby bat

screamed out in fright,

'Turn on the dark

I'm afraid of the light.'"

After that, Albert Blunt took out every single book about bats from the school library.

That must be how learning works!

Mrs. Windbag had a lot to learn about kindergarten.

She needed some help in the reading out loud department. So I made a suggestion.

"Take your time to savor each word, Mrs. Windbag,"

I said gently, and in private, just like Mrs. Ampersand used to tell me.

On Friday, when it should have been Popsicle time, because we'd tried hard all week, Mrs. Windbag brought in the most gross, grown-up foods you could ever gag on: asparagus, artichokes, and anchovies. "These are my favorite foods," she said.

We tasted them because Mrs. Ampersand always said we should try new things.

Truthfully, even my dog wouldn't have tried the anchovies.

You won't believe what Mrs. Windbag did on Monday, though. She brought in lemonade and a big pizza cookie!

Mrs. Ampersand always told us, 'Everyone makes mistakes. It's all about fixing them.'

While we ate our treat, Mrs. Windbag talked about our Graduation Day next week.

"I would like you to think about and share your most memorable moments in kindergarten," she explained.

"I will be playing my bagpipes to celebrate the big day."

Then she showed us a picture of her riding in a hot air balloon.

"It was very memorable!"

Mrs. Windbag was trying hard not to be boring. I could tell.

So I asked my mom if she could help me bring in Popsicles for Mrs. Windbag.

"That's using your noodle," Mom said.

On Graduation Day, everyone was all dressed up.

We walked across the stage to Mrs. Windbag's music. Look who was first! Oliver Crumb.

"I can count backward from five hundred!" he said.

"It was exciting when I learned that bats had babies like people," said Albert Blunt.

"I want to be an inventor like Thomas Edison when I grow up," said Marian Saltpeter.

Then it was my turn.

"I will never forget how sad I felt when I realized that Mrs. Ampersand wouldn't be my teacher anymore. So I started practicing to be just like her. I would like you to meet: Mabel Beecher, Future Teacher—Me!"

After the last kindergartener spoke, everyone applauded thunderously.

And guess who I saw in the audience! MRS. AMPERSAND! And there was her new baby!

Then Mrs. Windbag invited us all to a party in honor of us—even Mrs. Ampersand. There was whipped creamy cake and three kinds of grown-up gelato: pomegranate, mocha java, and pistachio.

Which were all delicious, by the way. I tried them.

"Did you know that the tip of your tongue is for tasting sweets?" I asked everyone, winking at Mrs. Ampersand. She winked back at me.

And you won't believe this, either! Mrs. Ampersand let me hold her baby, Andy. That was my second most memorable moment in kindergarten!

I'll teach him everything I know.